SEA OF GLASS

TRICIA D. WAGNER

LYRIDAE BOOKS

PRAISE FOR TRICIA D. WAGNER

*In **Sea of Glass**, Tricia D. Wagner weaves a brilliant story for the ages. **I can imagine it being told by generation after generation around a fire.** She is an accomplished writer and an extraordinary storyteller.*
- Nick Chiarkas, author of *Weepers*

*Wagner weaves a beautiful, heartbreaking yet hope-infused tale using enjoyably poetic writing. Imagery of the magnificent power of the sea as well as its calming beauty further enhance the story, mirroring the characters at times. **It was easy to lose myself within the elegance of Wagner's prose without losing any thrill for the plot or characters.***
- LT Ward

Wagner's ability to create a setting is breathtaking. I feel like I've been to these places. Her main characters are often children, which lets her explore deep themes in a very raw, unvarnished way.
- J Bacon

*Sea of Glass has **a cinematic quality** that allows readers to create memorable scenes that remain with them after the book is finished. I am looking forward to her next novel.*
- J Kantner

To my philosopher whose every word teaches.
Every day with you is music.

~

And to you
who stand with me on shore,
overlooking the deep sky and water,
our wings arcing, ready for flight.

The sky where we live
is no place to lose your wings.
So love, love, love.

Hafiz

SEA OF GLASS

Teo tapped the last nail in the window frame and stepped back. He studied his work—tight seams. Even plumb. The pane clean and full of Baja's blue ocean rolling behind him.

Hanging windows on shanties was heavy, hot work, and Papá griped that Teo hindered more than he helped. But in truth, Teo was getting good at this. And that was something, at just twelve.

Papá rounded the house and shooed Teo away.

Papá felt about the edges of the window.

He laid his level on top of the frame. Inspected each corner.

He found a bent nail that Teo had wedged in. "You've damaged the wood here."

"There was a knot."

"There will always be knots." Papá wrenched out the nail. "Hand me a new one."

Teo crouched by the tools, his gaze catching on the fresh window, reflecting the bay.

The burnished sun bled into lively waves, deepening their blues, softening their whites.

The angle of the glass set off a prism effect, making Papá look blurred, and it stretched a flicker of waves across his own image until he looked like a boy made of beating oceans. The reflection was so bright, it hid the bruise on his cheek.

Papá knocking Teo's shoulder broke the trance. "A nail."

Teo dug one from among the tools and handed it over, then slipped again into staring, rooting to find the illusion of the ocean in himself—ghosted.

Papá caught Teo's gaze in the window.

Teo stilled at the heat of those red eyes right on him.

There'd been a boy—Rafael, Teo's best friend and neighbor— last winter beaten and given to the sea.

Some said he walked the beach still, trekking the edge of the wash, looking at shells.

The Sea Angel, a spirit sacred in Mayan myths, supposedly looked after those lost at sea and would carry their spirits to Heaven.

But it seemed she'd forgotten Rafael.

Saúl, Teo's best friend remaining, had spotted Rafael's ghost— bruised and cold-looking. Alone.

Bruises from Papá always seemed to catch fire when he stared like this. Teo tried to ignore the hot itch of the one on his cheek— calling attention to it felt unwise—but he couldn't shake the tingle and rubbed it quick.

Papá glanced at the tools. "Daydreaming won't pack the supplies."

"I wasn't." Teo gathered hammers and nails. "I was just keeping an eye out."

Papá watched him a second too long. He didn't believe in ghosts, and he called Rafael's death "fate." And Rafael's father, who'd fled, Papá missed. It seemed, sometimes, Papá might know where he'd gone.

"Keeping an eye out for what?" asked Papá.

"I don't know. Ghosts."

"I've told you—forget him." Papá lifted the sack and started up the trail. "He's history."

Rafael wasn't history.

His death had rocked the whole barrio, and things still felt off. Anytime Teo looked at the ocean, Rafael's memory surfaced. Rafael and his father had worked off the coast as crab trappers, and he'd known everything about Breaker Bay.

He taught Teo to catch burrowing mollusks—how to see the invisible.

His death felt alive.

Papá waved him on. "It's time you leave off with your ghosts and such foolishness."

Teo followed him. "You say ghosts aren't real, yet you believe in the Sea Angel."

"That's no belief," said Papá. "The Sea Angel's sharp fact."

Saúl's papá said stories of the Sea Angel were just stories; that it was unwise to count on an angel to bring any change.

But most people feared her. Indeed, if a boy passed the harbor at sunset when the fishermen docked, those black-bearded sea ramblers would readily tell bloodied accounts of the Sea Angel delivering justice.

Papá turned the corner into a neighborhood that wasn't theirs.

They weren't going home, then.

They'd visit the old angler who gave Papá a cold one whenever they passed.

Teo started to follow, but a stinging on his foot stalled him. He crouched at the trail's edge.

Baja's summer sun would set the trails sizzling and sear his feet. In winter, the trails would cool and trap ocean mists, and the bottoms of bare feet would rupture and peel.

His beach feet were thick now, but a cut had split the callous of his instep.

He wiped a bead of blood.

Papá turned. Glimpsed the blood on him. "What'd you do?"

Glass usually made thin, even nicks that would bleed profusely. Then the bleeding would finish in a tender red line, sealed like lips. There wasn't much blood here.

"It's nothing. I must've just stepped on some glass."

Papá set down the tools and knelt. "Give it here."

Teo set his heel on Papá's knee.

Papá twisted his foot toward a porch light on a near shanty. He squeezed the cut.

White pain flashed.

Teo jerked in his leg.

Papá snatched his foot and slid pliers from the tool sack. "Hold still."

"What are you doing? There's no glass in it."

"A big piece, impacted. You shouldn't have walked on this." Papá spread the pliers.

Tears flashed. Any glass hurt to take out, but a big piece meant treacherous pain.

"Don't—I can do it." He coiled in his foot and crawled away.

Papá trapped his ankle in the crook of his arm.

There's a place—not of calm, but of resignation—whose doorway Teo had found the first time Papá struck him.

Entering it didn't lessen the horror, but it was an elsewhere place. Somewhere to be rather than here, meeting those iron hands, those red eyes.

Papá prodded the cut.

Teo cried out but didn't move. He just kept his gaze on the gritty ground. He felt the glass now. It seemed to be digging in under the fingers and pliers. A twist of Papá's hand and a rip.

Teo opened his eyes and found himself on his elbows, his mouth making a silent scream. The pain was an ink in his vision that cleared.

Papá tossed a bloody shard under his nose. "You need to watch where you step."

Teo got to his feet and stared at the ocean, letting his face dry.

He saw no ghost, but the whole bay seemed darkened by the sense of Rafael, standing someplace in the shallows, lifting his eyes from his shell, watching his best friend—blood on him—needing deliverance too.

Papá glanced back. "Time to go."

Teo kept his gaze on the water. "Saúl says the dead really do sometimes linger."

Papá's fingers twitched against his pocket, where lay a ring Mother once wore. "The dead want for nothing." He walked on, toward a door opening. "The dead are just dead."

Teo tried stepping.

The cut was sore, but he could walk.

The old angler, crooked but bright in the face, hashed with a raggedy grin, stumbled from his doorway. "What's all this talk at my threshold of ghouls?"

Papá ran an admiring hand along the rim of a window he'd hung on the man's house. "Don't mind the boy. His questions will tax you to death."

"Bah—questions are no tax," said the angler. "If we don't ask, we don't know."

Icons of the Sea Angel glinted across the man's walls, and candlelight streaming set off the planks in bright colors.

She was known to descend on her Day of Purification—tomorrow. The angler, it would seem, was prepared.

"Do you believe the Sea Angel really will come?" asked Teo.

Saúl, though not a month older than Teo, knew everything about angels and ghosts, and he said she would. Saúl and his grandmother had spied the Sea Angel on past holy days.

"Why, yes—though, it's a matter of faith," said the angler. "She watches over her own and goes after those troubling her waters. Delivers gifts to the kindhearted. Deals curses on those desecrating what's hers. She offers healing and freedom and justice to everyone."

"Everyone?" asked Teo. "To Rafael, even?"

Papá eased past the angler, inside. "You don't have to entertain this."

The angler gave Papá a beer. "She keeps souls, dead and living. Burnt offerings—powerful rites—drew her eye in ancient times. Now, more, it takes faith. Someday, I'll teach you to pray."

The angler seemed sincere, but the second Papá sat, the door shut, leaving Teo in the cooling twilight while the men settled in with their bottles.

Teo walked along the trail sloping to the beach.

The wind was up now, and the stinging on his foot was a bother. But at the bight of the cliffs, scrambling among boulders—Saúl.

The Sea Angel keeping the dead and the living…coming tomorrow…

It didn't matter if the angler hadn't taught Teo to pray. Saúl knew how.

Teo set in a run.

They could offer up prayers to the Sea Angel for Rafael, and she'd unshackle his ghost from the Bay.

Teo scaled down to the sand, tiptoeing among snowy plover nests—little divots woven of beach sundries and trash.

Saúl waved from a boulder's top and hopped down.

Teo sprinted until they stood facing each other.

It was always odd for a moment, encountering Saúl.

Three don't easily become two, and even now, when they met, they both glanced at the water, as though waiting for Rafael to trip out of the shallows and run to them.

"The old angler believes that the Sea Angel's coming tomorrow," said Teo.

"Of course she's coming," said Saúl.

"I was thinking—if Rafael's trapped in the bay as a ghost, we could ask her to save him."

"Would she? Rafael's…you know…dead."

"The angler says she'll help anyone. If you really do know how to pray, we can try."

"I do know how. Grandmother says the Sea Angel's drawn to the requests of those bringing tributes of special beauty. We'd have to offer them in a holy place on the coast." Saúl glanced north. "Her Hollow might work."

"Or, we could try a ritual of ancient times," said Teo.

Teo glanced at the birds' nests.

Most nests spangling the beach were abandoned, but some cradled dead, pink-skinned fledglings—wet, freshly eggless babies whose hunted parents had abandoned them.

"The angler called burnt offerings *powerful rites*," said Teo.

All pinions and raw skin, the baby birds seemed to ache. To ease that, he'd burned them before.

"We could light a fledgling on fire and pray over the smoke."

A nest by them was heavy with a carcass. Pot-bellied and pencil-necked, opaquely transparent and featherless—the hatchling was wretched.

"Grandmother calls burning the dead a desecration," said Saúl.

The burning of the dead was something Papá feared too, and he always seemed wise to what Teo was up to—by a waft of foul scent, by a speck of ash on his hand.

But burning the birds felt like performing a rescue. It seemed understandable why a goddess might want that.

From the top of the cliffs, a man, his face rutilant in the pink and gold of the going sun, waved.

It was Saúl's Papá, Señor Felipe.

"Meet me at dawn with your tribute." Saúl backed to the cliff. "If she comes, this is the last night Rafael will be cold."

Teo set to trolling the beach, searching for something of special beauty he could offer. He stopped at spotting three silky, almost-spherical quartz stones, shining from the sand like a clutch of glass eggs.

Wet with mist, pale under twilight, they glowed like moonstones. A good tribute.

He slipped them inside his pocket.

As the evening deepened to indigo, Papá's stumbling shadow appeared, backlit by radiance streaming from the angler's house. Teo climbed up to him and followed him home.

Papá shoved open their door and herded Teo in. He quaffed the dregs of his bottle and sank into a rocking chair. Papá looked wrong in that chair. It was suited for Mother.

Teo fastened the windows and roused a flickering fire. He drew out the three tribute stones and set them before the blaze.

Light swelled them—flashed, like living starlight skittering over the walls.

"Like an angel approaching," he whispered.

Papá pointed the neck of his bottle at him. "You want tales of the Sea Angel? Sit."

Teo crouched before the chair. As little as it seemed Papá could understand such things, he did believe them, and he might've picked up something helpful.

"Some say the Sea Angel spirits people away," said Teo. "Does she?"

"She does indeed take folk." Papá kept his gaze low. "She's of wrath more than mercy."

Huddling at the foot of Mother's chair, listening to it creak, felt like lingering at the threshold of a doorway that kept her.

Papá rocked, muttering dark tales as the window bled black. Stories eerie and harrowing.

The Sea Angel, dripping with water and tears, rising from the ocean.

Storm winds stirred by her fingers to break ships and bodies.

Lost sailors transformed into hideous fishes.

As the fire died, Papá's murmuring shifted to snoring.

Teo laid his blanket bundle near the window, where he'd hear the fishing gulls calling at dawn.

Though he slept fitfully, comfort crept in.

This was the last night Rafael would be alone.

Tomorrow, the Sea Angel would spirit him off, or change him, or—something.

On the back of that solace, a sorrow arrived.

It felt almost like jealousy.

But how could he feel jealous? Rafael was on the brink of peace—that was glad.

He flipped over and lay on his unbruised cheek. That was better. Unbruised. That's what Rafael soon would be.

When night finally lifted, the gulls took flight and sang to the darkling east.

The black sky was bluing with the pressure of the sun, and though the darkness seemed heavy as iron, the sun was persistent, and night would soon break like the shell of an egg, transforming the shivery dawn into a streaming, yellow morning.

Teo pried open the shanty's side window and pushed the pane until there yawned a gap big enough to slip through. The front door tended to stick and would squeal, but the window would swing without making a sound.

Teo slipped the three silky, spherical stones into his pocket alongside his matches.

Artful as a shore crab, he shimmied out without scraping his sides or catching his shorts.

As he dropped onto the sandy earth, the slice from his glass sliver smarted.

His foot was bleeding again, but not much.

He spied through the window at Papá, still passed out in Mother's chair.

A gray flash of wing swooped. Teo spun—

A storm petrel.

It climbed the sky on columns of wind, then joined a troupe dancing on waves, its flight effortless. Spirit-like.

It had only to stretch its blades of wings, shaping them like main moonsails, and the sea winds would carry it high over waters.

Teo fastened the window. Sealing it felt like clipping a thread that'd kept his shoulders bent.

He spread his arms and took off, the whole coast spreading before him seeming to await the Sea Angel. He wove down trails to the planar expanse of the Beach of Palms.

In the holiness of dawn's quiet, the owl limpet shells seemed to belong to the Sea Angel. So did the winds, ruffling the silhouetted snowy plovers. And the silver waves, beating from blue ocean trenches to Baja's fine sands.

Soon, Rafael would belong to her, too.

When Teo reached the waterline, he gazed east along a narrow pathway weaving through the garbage mound, up and among the inland shanties where Saúl lived.

Flashes of morning glanced off a blue-black head rounding the bend of the barrio.

Teo took the sand trail at a run and stopped before Saúl. "What'd you bring?"

Saúl turned out his pocket, revealing a glistening handful of sea glass. "Can't beat that, I bet."

"I found the best tribute." Teo produced his stones, tumbled smooth by waves that'd been churning them in tidal intervals on and off the shore for several millennia.

"Those are worthless. They're just rocks."

Teo rubbed his thumb over his stones. They'd seemed special at twilight, so glossy, almost perfectly round. But out of the wash, bone-dry, they did look sort of common.

"What if she knows, already, that Rafael needs her?" asked Teo. "This might be enough."

Saúl shrugged. "We can try."

Over the ridge to the south, the roofline of Papá's shanty loomed.

Teo stepped back and pitched one of his stones high and far, straight at the shanty.

It curved away west in an upsweep of wind. He raised another, tested its weight, and let it fly.

The stone tumbled through the sun-heavy air, quartz facets glinting. It struck the ridge and rolled, stirring a parched concoction of yellow earth and salt sand.

Teo readied the last stone for a colossal throw.

Saúl caught his arm. "You'll wake your papá. He'll bruise you."

The thought of landing that stone on Papá's shanty felt so good. "He'll bruise me anyway."

Teo cocked his arm.

Saúl grabbed Teo's wrist, fingered the stone from his fist, and cast it at the ocean.

The stone plunked and drew concentric rings before a frothy wave gobbled the water.

Teo backed off from Saúl. "The Sea Angel goes after people who trouble her waters."

Saúl raced past. "Better run!"

Teo limped after him but stumbled to a halt. He was the fastest runner in the barrio and could usually best Saúl, but the instep of his foot ached. Saúl, far off, waved.

Teo managed the last of the distance by hopping on his good foot.

They crept across a craggy ledge made passable by thick mats of seaweed, then together stood before a brink that plunged fifteen feet into the shore—Sea Angel's Hollow.

Sea Angel's Hollow was an intertidal crevasse that bubbled over with ocean when the water was high. With dawn had come a low tide, and the Hollow was parching. The interior was perfectly round, which made it feel holy.

Without a doubt, this belonged to the Sea Angel, for here, many times, they'd found gifts.

The first was a tangle of dying jellyfish, evidently cast over the Hollow's edge at the height of a summer storm.

Saúl and Teo had wanted to throw them back, but Rafael knew better than to touch them, and he made them keep clear.

The three boys crouched around the slick mass for a whole afternoon, watching glassy tentacles slither until they finally dehydrated.

Another time, when Teo visited the Hollow alone, he found a catshark egg case.

It was the length of his hand and smooth as glass.

Sewn inside was a near-born baby shark whose wriggling Teo could feel. The case was still soppy, but its edges were dry. Teo hurried it to the ridge, wedged it in his shirt, and dived.

The shark sewn inside livened as Teo ferried it into deepening, heavily pressured waters.

The smell of sea depths, maybe, or the growing chill, made the unborn creature wild until it thrashed in its case like it was the ocean's beating heart.

Teo leapt down the Hollow, following a familiar course of cemented barnacles and ragged holes drilled by the teeth of snails. Saúl dropped beside him and crouched.

Teo, having nothing to offer, edged closer to him.

Saúl handed Teo the glass. "We can pray for you, too, you know. For the Sea Angel to get you free of your papá."

"Could that actually happen?" No boy could survive Breaker Bay on his own.

"Why not?" asked Saúl. "She helps everyone. Maybe she'd make you a spirit or something."

Hope washed in a flurry of images—himself, a spirit, splashing the shallows beside Rafael, the Sea Angel leading them someplace they never would feel fear or bleed.

Would she take him? Or change him?

Summoning her for himself might really mean transforming into a spirit—but so?

Spirits don't carry bruises.

"What about you?" asked Teo. "If she took me and Rafael, both, you'd be the one left alone."

"I wouldn't be alone," said Saúl. "My papá's okay."

Teo pressed the sand flat, then situated the frosted bottle shards, making a stained-glass window on the seabed. "Is this a special enough tribute to draw her?"

Saúl blew sand off the sea glass. "It looks pretty good."

The powerful rites, though.

"What if fire really could make it better?" Teo pulled his book of matches from his pocket and lit one. He stood it like a candle at the center of the tribute.

The small flame burned hot and fast, its glow glancing off the shards and glittering their skin blue and green.

The match snuffed at its base and sent a tendril of smoke twisting into the sky.

"That ought to do it!" said Saúl.

"Should we say something?" asked Teo.

"Just think of him," said Saúl. "Think of the Sea Angel rescuing him. And you too."

The images flitting seemed too good to hope for. She'd look at the bruise on his cheek, the way Mother used to. And she'd... well...whatever she'd do, it'd be great.

Saúl led Teo out of the Hollow.

The risen sun had lifted the mist off the sea, showing a horizon on all sides distant and clear.

"Is she coming?" asked Teo.

"She must be. See how calm the sea suddenly looks? Even the deeps will obey her."

The sea did look calm.

Well, calmer.

Waves still roared, but the wind had eased.

"When you saw her, what'd she look like?" asked Teo.

Saúl shrugged. "I guess—my mother."

"And Rafael? When you saw him, did he look…dead?"

"He looked just like himself. Bruised. Wading the shallows."

The water shifted from blue to gray.

The wind lifted and died.

A bank of clouds soared in and left.

Nobody, angel or otherwise, visited the coast.

No boy waded the shallows.

Saúl stood. "I've gotta go."

"You don't want to see this?" asked Teo.

"It seems she's not coming. And there's no sign of Rafael's ghost."

Teo studied the beach, north to south. "She has to come."

Saúl glanced at the backshore. "Well, the baby will wake Mother soon. I have to get back before then, or it'll be more chores. Shouldn't you leave, too? Your papá will look for you."

Leaving meant doubting the Sea Angel.

Leaving meant spending the day dodging Papá, red-eyed from drink and put out by some trivial offense. And not just this day. All days.

It was either let the Sea Angel make him a spirit or let Papá make him a ghost.

"I'm staying."

Saúl started off but paused. "If she turns you into spirit, promise to visit? We can play tricks on the fishermen." He crept off, over the weedy stones, then raced toward the barrio.

Teo trekked toward the water, where he could better see something coming. He settled on a boulder by the sea and plunged in his foot, sinking it to the level of silt.

He dragged his cut through the muck, muting a deep itch.

The sand brushing it felt healthy. What was glass anyway, but sand? Perhaps the Sea Angel, commanding the ocean, would seam him closed, seal him like the rim of a catshark egg case.

The wind's whispering suddenly sounded like a hushed choir. Teo studied the waves.

The ocean's roar softened, like a panther deferring to something more dreadful approaching.

This had to be it. This had to be the preamble to the Sea Angel's coming.

A thunder of gray whales plunged in from the south, ushering a pod of giant calves—hungry, playing, plowing tracks through the water. They sailed through like a choir of foghorns, blowing lungfuls of bubbly sea at the birds.

Teo watched until the whales moved off. He watched, his foot's ache shrilling into a sting, until the winds stagnated in the heat of high morning. Three boats seeped over the southern horizon and slipped north.

A passing cloud glittered him with goosebumps.

Had that been her?

Teo studied his hands, his arms, watching for the glinting of blue and green—of gold—like the dancing flames cast. Was he tending spirit-ward? Or fish-like?

Teo hurried to the Hollow and looked over the brink. The tribute still sparkled, untaken. He touched his cheek. The bruise there still smarted. A trickle of blood warmed his foot.

He rubbed his bruise as he wandered back to the waterline.

Was his sea glass not special? Was the Sea Angel watching, fully knowing about Papá and not caring? Would she forsake Rafael? That couldn't be right. Maybe she didn't want tributes.

He stopped before the nest of a cold baby bird.

The old rituals. The powerful rites. Burnt offerings summoning her in the dark days before prayers.

He scooped up the bird—frigid and shining so pink it seemed cobbled of quartz. Tiny organs in reds, blues, and yellows—bruise-toned—showed beneath cages of fragile bones. Its bulges of eyes, shielded by membranes, looked sleeping. The wings rested folded.

Teo gathered a pile of kindling sticks. He struck a match, lit the tinder, and blew the sparks into a twisting flame.

This might be desecration, but was it not also a sort of redemption? A bold sending off by way of smoke to let the bird finally fly?

He felt the bird's tender foot, curling and tipped with claws sharp as slivers. He half-expected the baby to rouse at the touch.

He laid it on the pyre.

The fire stretched its fingers, shedding sparks and puffs as it drummed the kindling.

The shadows cast by the blaze looked like skirts; the tongues of fire—locks of hair. The burn ignited a last handful of sticks, then sank into a brooding heap of flames, withdrawing into its hot, blue belly, curling its golden fingers around the body of the bird.

The beak charred. The fire died. Blood tickled Teo's foot. He stomped it and stared at the tendrils of woodsmoke unspooling.

No one came out of the water. No one came out of the sky.

No one floated along the beach. No beautiful mother manifesting from nothing, as though she were let out of Heaven.

Teo dug into the fire with a pair of sticks and pinched the beak and legs.

He ought to bury what was left. Burying the bones in the Hollow—maybe the Sea Angel would spirit the baby away and let it soar—a splashy halcyon bird to brighten Rafael's sky. He blew the remains cool.

"You've burned kindling, and not brought it for cooking?"

Teo spun.

Papá, backlit by the sun.

Teo staggered. Glanced at the water.

No angel.

"Out wasting time, when no breakfast is cooked." Papá advanced. "By now, you should've collected the kindling."

Teo skittered back. "I did collect kindling." Blood dribbling under his foot left a stain.

Papá focused on Teo's hand—sooted.

His fingers knotted. "What are you hiding?"

Teo produced the ashy remnants of his bird.

"I've told you to leave such things alone." Papá swung.

Teo wheeled back.

"A boy who'll not learn must pay." Papá tripped. Righted himself.

Teo searched the desolate sky.

"Let go of that filth and get to the shanty. I'll deal with you there."

Teo glanced at the water, the shallows. "I'm not coming with you." He closed his hand tightly around the bird.

Papá hung still, as though dizzied, his gaze tracing Teo's blood-streaked foot. "You'll go wash your foot in the ocean. Then you'll come straight home."

"I won't!"

Teo bolted, leaping clusters of grass, skirting rocks, limping when he had to. He ran until his foot was on fire.

Finally, he slowed and glanced back.

Papá held his gaze a moment, then set to climbing the rise, toward the shanty.

Teo crouched near the wash and fought to catch his breath.

Before him lay a tattered nest, jumbled with broken eggs. No carcasses.

These babies might've discovered they had wings and lifted into a sunsetted sky. Or, perhaps the raptors had already visited, impaling the fledglings' tender skin, imprinting bruises with terrible talons.

Among the split shells, something shone.

Teo dug out a glossy quartz stone, half-buried. It was rosy-translucent and heavy.

He retraced his steps until he could see Papá's shanty. Even at this distance, it seemed he could smell beer.

He cocked his arm way back and launched the stone.

The droning of waves splintered with the sparkle of a rupturing window.

Teo beat it down the beach, gulls wheeling. He hopped across seaweed mats to the Hollow and climbed down. He crooked on the dry sand beside the glass tribute.

Breaker Bay no longer seemed to belong to the Sea Angel. The whole coast felt like Papá's.

But he was not Papá's. It was as if by shattering the window, he'd not just snapped a thread but severed a tether.

Clouds sailed in, casting the Hollow in shade like the interior swirl of a barren conch—a place forgotten or wholly unknown.

Teo laid the charred bird on the sea glass.

The blue shards made a good semblance of ocean sky.

The browns felt like the coming of night. The body looked like a silhouette of a soaring bird, crossing a twilit sea.

Teo gathered damp sand by handfuls and buried it.

The damp clumps cast a chill, like he was sprinkling burial earth on his own body.

He stared up at the Hollow's rim.

At the Hollow enveloping him, dousing him in quiet, an illusion of safety settled.

But this place was not safe. Papá knew that he came here.

Teo climbed out and hunkered on the beach, low among boulders, until the sun coasted overhead—a golden bird burning through a kindling of clouds.

Where to go? Where would Papá not find him?

The old angler's house. Papá knew Teo hated the place—he'd never look there. And the angler knew how to pray.

If he could just make it there without being sighted—he'd hide there until evening, then leave before Papá might come for a drink.

Teo snuck to the barrio through the rough, ducking behind scrub at each trail.

When he reached the house, he pounded on the door.

The angler opened it. "Why, what's got hold of you? You look as sallow as stormwater."

"May I come in? Papá can't know I'm here."

The angler glanced at the bruised cheek, then stepped aside. "Did you seek the Sea Angel?"

Teo slipped in. "I tried tributes. Burnt offerings, even. Nothing worked. You said you'd teach me to pray. If you do, I might still catch her."

"One doesn't 'catch' the Sea Angel." The angler settled down at a table. "She answers or doesn't, according to her will."

"Our tribute was great, and it should've been more than acceptable."

"It isn't about tributes." The angler pulled out a chair for him. "The point is, angels are all-knowing, whereas we know little. If the Sea Angel chose not to answer your prayer, she had reasons. Keep seeking and one day, you'll surely understand."

Teo sat. "How can the Sea Angel be all knowing? She forgot Rafael."

"Mysterious are the ways of gods and angels—all powerful," said the angler. "We mortals can't fathom their workings."

"So, gods and angels have all the knowledge and all of the power, and yet they won't help us? You can't believe that."

"Do you imagine yourself more than mortal, that you'd question the work of those holy?"

Teo stared through the man's pure window at the swallowing sea, tending sapphiric in the lowering, westbound sun. "Believe me, I know that I'm mortal."

The angler fixed his hoary eyes on Teo. "Praying neither changes the gods nor the difficulties we face. This world—it is what it is."

Teo staggered at those old eyes, looking on him, bruised, yet seeing nothing beyond their own passivity.

The angler was great in years and still worked his fishing ship.

He was capable of action, of strength, of wisdom—yet he was resigned.

"What's the point in praying, if it changes nothing?" asked Teo.

"We people may have little power. But you see, when we pray, we change our acceptance of things; our level of strength to bear pain."

Teo stood. "If anything needs changing, it's Papá."

"Calm yourself. Listen. I'll speak of the Sea Angel. Of what it means to be her subject."

"But I don't want to be a subject—I want to be a son." Teo tripped back, knocking over his chair. "You know what Papá's like. Yet you send him home stumbling."

The old man sat dumb, as though fiddling through platitudes to come up with the right one. "Your papá's a lost lamb. Many men are. The Sea Angel knows and will work for the best."

"Rafael's death—it wasn't for the best."

"We can't see the whole picture."

"My mother's death, then. Are you saying she ought to have died?"

"Sad, indeed," said the angler. "Yet look how you're seeking the holy things, now."

"What about my own death?" asked Teo.

"By death, even, we might grow in faith. We can't see all ends. Trust the gods, the Sea Angel, to bring forth what's good."

The sun dipped into the window, blazing bright the garish emblems hanging. Emblems of paper and foil, framed pictures: pristine bottled goddesses, impotent.

"If there are gods and angels, they're nothing like this. Real ones would hate what my papá's become. Real ones would change things."

The angler cast his gaze toward a dusty book—the Sea Angel glaring from its cover—as though it would slip him an answer.

He tore out a page. "A prayer for the brokenhearted. Speak it when you've calmed."

Teo pocketed the prayer. "You can't tell Papá I've been here."

The angler glanced at Teo's foot. "Your own blood may betray you."

Teo blotted blood from the floor, then tied up his foot.

He peeked out the door, then slipped into the brush. He ducked down the cliff and kept in thick cover as he hiked to the waterline.

He climbed the ocean-side of a boulder as the sun touched the surf.

Soon the sky would shift black, and the water and coast. He'd sneak into town and find something to eat, and then—what?

At his feet, water rushing in, drawing back, left patterns of cyclonic sand. Out of it, tiny bubbles rose. Popped. Teo spaded a handful of soppy sand, unburdening it of its secrets—

A herd of burrowing mollusks slipped out, their shells flashing fiery likes gemstones.

They twisted before him an instant, then vanished.

Going after truth and things holy—if it could just be like this. If he could just learn, like Rafael had taught him, to see what's invisible, the burden of Papá would lift, and he'd find himself in the company of gods.

But things as they were—the bleak sea, bearing nothing but nothing; the vacant sky, bringing no change. It hung as a deadweight.

That mirrored reflection he'd seen of himself in the bay—it was as though he were already a ghost. Powerless. Lingering. Waiting. Unseen.

He unfolded the prayer for the brokenhearted.

The prayer was long and meandering and had little point.

Whoever had written it seemed not to know what brokenheartedness felt like.

Teo studied his hands holding the page.

His fingers were calloused and sure, the prayer they held babbling.

If there were gods, they'd have hands with callouses—hardworking hands, yet tender. Liable to bleed.

They'd have hands prone to hold the cold fledglings. To help them.

Teo stayed in the crook of the boulder until sunbeams painted him and the boulder alike, until he felt blended with it, until the burn in his foot was true pain.

He glanced out, again and again, fearing each moment to sight Papá coming.

Finally, the sun crashed into the sea, setting fire to the mist—a frigid golden blanket.

When the water swallowed the last of the rays, under a dusting of twilight, Teo crept onto the beach.

Papá was nowhere in sight, but he certainly would be out, if not drinking, then looking.

Teo slipped along a trail weaving among shanties. From the higher bends, he paused to keep watch.

The copper sky steeled, and the western winds rose, pressing a gray mist that darkened the streets.

The wind carried a baby's wailing from the north end of the Barrio.

Teo walked gingerly against his foot's ache toward the sound until he reached the doorway of Saúl's shanty.

Saúl wasn't inside—just his mother was, holding his gently crying newborn sister. A little candle flickered on a driftwood table.

There were no windows hung here—just curtained holes cut for light.

Chilly clouds shrouded the fallen night. The mist, riding a steady wind, pushed past him, in.

The baby's weeping was pain.

For this—even this—would an angel not come?

This mess of decrepit shanties; the body-strewn beach; the barrio's garbage mound dark against stars—Breaker Bay was a forsaken place.

Nothing, not even the burning of the dead, could be a desecration here. How can you desecrate what's already forgotten by those things that call themselves holy?

The wind swelled the flame.

The baby's cry sharpened.

Teo gazed toward the Hollow.

Feeling its vacancy, the non-existence of the Sea Angel there, the non-existence of angels in Breaker Bay—it was like a crack splitting a shell.

The coastal mists hung heavy with the unshakable sense of Rafael, his presence seeming to blend with his absence in an irreconcilable way.

Yet the sand by the sea—empty and glazed firm by waves—hid whole worlds. And the night sky shone a baleful blue waxing starry.

Teo stared at the mist sliding in and tried to picture what might lay behind it. Not the Sea Angel, chintzy in sequins and tinselly robes. But a real god with real hands. A real god, aching for change. A real god who'd keep him, despite whether he knew how to pray.

Teo hurried off, no longer limping, but taking the trail to the garbage mound at a run.

He ignored his cut's throb while he trawled through the rubbish.

He pried loose pine planks from a splintering door frame, still suitable. He picked up nails as they presented themselves. He found a block of wood sturdy enough to make a decent hammer.

The rising moon glinted in winks that betrayed hidden panels of glass.

He scavenged until he found a whole remnant wall of a dilapidated shanty, most of its glass still intact.

He liberated a pane, easing its broken frame away with a wedge of wood.

He hurried back into the barrio, carrying wood and glass across his back, the baby's cry guiding him along dark trails.

When he reached Saúl's shanty, the candle was cold. The baby was wailing out of the indigo gloom, her mother fruitlessly shushing her.

Teo got to work at once measuring the opening.

He cobbled a frame, taking the heads of nails from between his teeth and hammering them with his plank.

The shushing stopped. The mother's dark eyes, shining by moonlight, watched him.

He held the frame to the starry sky, considering its plumb. The wood was rotted on one corner, but still, it was a good frame.

He slid in the glass and tacked it in place. He raised the new window and hung it.

The sharp wind glanced off and spun quietly away.

A strike of light leapt on the table, and there was Saúl's papá, Señor Felipe, holding a match to the candle. He shook out the spark and waved: *come.*

Teo didn't hesitate. There was only ever kindness in the face of Saúl's papá.

"What a service you've done us," said Señor Felipe. "What can I pay you?"

Teo glanced around the shanty.

Bags of grain and bottles of oil stood small and lean.

A cold stove rested alongside a sparse box of kindling.

An empty iron skillet slept on its grate.

"You don't have to pay me." Teo stomped against blood feathering his instep. "Where's Saúl?"

Señor Felipe knelt before Teo. "He's with his grandmother tonight."

Señor Felipe pointed at the blood stain on Teo's wrapped foot.

"What happened?"

"I stepped on some glass."

He lifted Teo's foot. "Did the glass come out?"

Teo pulled away. "I just need to put it in the ocean."

Señor Felipe guided Teo into a chair. "The ocean is dirty, child."

"Papá says seawater's good for glass cuts."

Señor Felipe, kneeling, cradling Teo's heel, shook his head. "Your papá." He rolled up his sleeves. "I can look at it, yes?"

Teo gripped the arms of the chair.

Señor Felipe removed the cloth. He ran his thumbs along Teo's foot, softly pressing his swollen instep. He whispered something to his wife.

She stepped out a moment, then returned with the baby tied to her back. She held a pitcher of water and a sewing basket.

Señor Felipe bathed Teo's foot, wetting his own lap too. He drew out a pair of scissors. "Close your eyes."

Teo bit his lip and readied for agony.

There was pressure, tugging, and then a gush.

Teo peeked.

Dark blood was dribbling from the center of his foot and down his heel, staining the man's tan pants.

Señor Felipe reached into the basket and drew out a needle.

Afraid he'd scream, Teo bit his tongue.

Señor Felipe touched the hottest part of the cut.

A tingling and a slip—and then night air relieving the burn.

"That must feel better," said Señor Felipe.

Teo winked open one eye, then the other. Señor Felipe was smiling, one fist resting on his hip.

Teo turned over his foot. Señor Felipe had opened his calloused sole, revealing a crescent-shaped cut, its bleeding tapering.

Señor Felipe laid aside a chunk of glass, triangular like the tooth of a shark. He bandaged the cut, then snugged Teo's foot in a bundle of clean sewing cloths. Saúl's mother tucked a blanket around Teo.

Teo gazed at the baby tied to her softly curving shoulders, her dark hair dusting the baby's face.

She mixed flour and oil and pressed dough into the pan.

In a moment, she was holding a hot tortilla against his palm, and he was biting it, his eyes hardly open.

Teo woke to the dawn cries of gulls.

He pushed away the blanket and tried to stand. There was no tickling itch, no burn. His foot just felt weakly bruised, like he'd stepped on a rock.

He peered through the window at the ocean, brightening to a pure, polished blue. By now, high tide would've brought frigid water tipping into the Hollow, saturating it with moony waves, hauling out the sea glass and the body of the bird.

Teo studied his hands. If hanging one window had taken the burden of tears from a baby, what might more do?

He crept past Saúl's sleeping parents, their two bodies making a nest for their baby bird. He lifted his hammering wedge and trekked over the ridge to the garbage mound.

In the shimmer of the dawning day, the hilled horizon sparkled like a sea of glass.

THE END

FREE EBOOK

Night Swiftly Falling
by Tricia D. Wagner

Eight-year-old Swift is lost in dreams of sea legends and pirate adventures, until an encounter with the deadly power of the ocean shocks him into reality. Swift struggles to hang onto his childhood fantasies, but his new understanding of the fragile nature of life and friendships threatens to swamp his hope. Under the guidance of his older brother, Caius, Swift must learn to brave the challenging waves of change without losing himself to their destruction.

To get your FREE eBook, visit:
www.TriciaWagner.com

ALSO BY TRICIA D. WAGNER

SWIFT & THE STAR OF ATLANTIS SERIES

A STARRY-EYED BOY. A CRYPTIC MAP. A MYTHICAL TREASURE.

WHAT PERILS AWAIT IN THE CHASING OF DREAMS?

AS SWIFT LIVES UP TO HIS NAME AND HIS FAMILY LEGACY, YOUNG ADULTS RECEIVE A FAST-PACED FANTASY THAT WILL APPEAL NOT JUST ON THE ADVENTURE OR FANTASY LEVELS, BUT IN MATTERS OF THE HEART AS THE YOUNG STRUGGLE FOR INDEPENDENCE AND ACTION IN THE FACE OF PARENTAL RESTRICTIONS. TRICIA D. WAGNER'S ATTENTION TO PAIRING PSYCHOLOGICAL STRUGGLE WITH THE ADVENTURE OF FINDING A PROMISED TREASURE CREATES A STORY THAT PULLS ON THE EMOTIONS OF YOUNG READERS AS IT SATISFIES THEIR DESIRE FOR ACTION AND ADVENTURE.

-D. Donovan, Senior Reviewer, *Midwest Book Review*

ALSO BY TRICIA D. WAGNER

A GIRL BRAVE ENOUGH TO DANCE MAY JUST FIND -

GRIEF SINKS AWAY THROUGH THE SOLES OF TAP SHOES.

*A DANCER. A CREATURE. A SPIRE-CAPPED AND LONELY BOARDING SCHOOL. **LITTLE GIRL CAN DANCE** IS A SPELLBINDING TALE TOLD OVER SIX SWEEPING ACTS. TRICIA D. WAGNER'S SIGNATURE STYLE IS ON TOP FORM IN THIS BEAUTIFUL NOVELLA.*

A WONDERFUL FUSION OF POETIC PROSE AND LIMITLESS IMAGINATION PLUNGES YOU STRAIGHT INTO ANDROMEDA'S MESMERISING WORLD.

PREPARE TO HAVE YOUR HEART BROKEN AND MENDED AGAIN IN THIS SHORT BUT STUNNING FABLE.

*-**ELEANOR HAWKEN**, AUTHOR OF THE BLUE LADY AND SAMMY FERAL'S DIARIES OF WEIRD*

ABOUT THE AUTHOR

TRICIA D. WAGNER IS AN AWARD-WINNING NOVELIST, POET, AND SHORT STORY WRITER. SHE GREW UP IN AMARILLO, TEXAS, CHASING STORMS, RIDING STALLIONS, SOJOURNING THROUGH PAINTED CANYONS, DISAPPEARING INTO FLOATING MESAS UNDER STARRY SKIES.

SHE NOW LIVES IN ROCKFORD, ILLINOIS (THOUGH THE TRUTH IS, SHE'S A CITIZEN OF A DOZEN FICTIONAL COUNTRIES). TRICIA WORKS IN EDUCATION AND LIVES DAY TO DAY WONDERSTRUCK BUT LUCKILY CAN FEEL HER WAY ABOUT THIS TERRIFYING, BEAUTIFUL EARTH THROUGH WRITING.

TRICIA HAS PIECES PUBLISHED IN THE *WRITE CITY MAGAZINE*, *CHICAGO NEWA*, *WORD OF ART 3D*, *LITERARY YARD*, AND *MIDWEST REVIEW*.

AUTHOR'S NOTE

I love connecting with readers and writers. If, you're interested in stories, then you're a kindred spirit to me, and I have lots more in store for you.

To quote another kindred spirit in writing, Jedi Master Stephen King:

"Writing is magic, as much as the water of life as any other art. The water is free. So drink. Drink and be filled up."

If you're interested not only in stories, but in story creation, visit my website and sign up to receive a FREE **Story Kickoff Character Worksheet.**

I designed this tool for that first moment of getting our feet wet at the brink of a story.

To get your FREE worksheet, visit:
www.TriciaWagner.com

ALSO BY TRICIA D. WAGNER

A SENSE OF BELONGING MAY ONLY COME

FROM ACCEPTING HOW DIFFERENT WE ARE.

TEN-YEAR-OLD SWIFT LONGS TO BE AS GROWN UP AS HIS BROTHERS, BUT IN CONFRONTING HIMSELF IN THE WILDS OF THE NORTH ATLANTIC, HE MUST CONTEND WITH WHAT IT MEANS TO BE A MAN.